Chocolate Moon

by

Mary Arrigan

First published in 2005 in Great Britain by
Barrington Stoke Ltd, Sandeman House, Trunk's Close,
55 High Street, Edinburgh EH1 1SR

ISBN 1-842992-93-7

Printed in Great Britain by Bell & Bain Ltd

A Note from the Author

My dad was my hero. When I was little he had answers for all my weird questions. He told me fantastic stories and made my life exciting and fun. Part of his job was to take away library books from houses where there were horrible illnesses like TB or polio. But my dad loved books so much he just couldn't bring himself to burn them. So he gave them to my brother and me and told us we might not live to the end of the book, we might catch TB or polio, too. There's nothing like a death threat to make a book more exciting.

Dad spoke Italian. He adored music and he could sing all the songs from every opera written by Verdi – if we let him. When I was a poor art student, Dad would buy my art books. He'd use book tokens he won (lots of times) for the *Sunday Times* prize crossword. He'd read the books and then argue with me about modern art.

When he began to forget things, we knew that, bit-by-bit, we were losing our brilliant father. He had Alzheimer's disease and was slipping away slowly into his own world.

I like to think my father is somewhere colourful, singing all those Verdi operas out of tune.

This book is for him.

In memory of my dad,
Brendan Nolan

Contents

Chapter 1
Gran

Sundays. I still don't like to think about those Sundays. Even now.

"Get a move on, Chris," Mum said. "We're leaving in ten minutes."

"I don't want to go."

"Chris!" shouted Dad. "What's got into you?"

Yes, sure, I *was* in a bad mood. But not because of going to see Gran.

At last, we'd all head for Saint Mark's Nursing Home, with bags of stupid stuff like grapes and magazines.

"It's mad bringing that stuff," I said. "You know Gran will put them in the bin as soon as we've left."

"Be quiet, Chris," said Mum. She shook her head and looked at Dad. They didn't like me making a big fuss.

They didn't know anything, did they? I knew that Gran wasn't bothered about fruit and presents. What made me feel bad was that she was never angry with Mum and Dad. I wanted her to scream and kick and act up. But no, she just sat and smiled and answered Mum and Dad's silly questions.

"How are you feeling?" Dad would say.

"Do you get out in the garden now that the weather's better?" Mum would ask.

"Bingo on Tuesdays? Isn't that fun!" they would say together.

Crap stuff like that. One day Gran said she was going to art classes and Mum and Dad nearly wet themselves with the excitement of having something new to talk to her about. Something that made *them* feel better. She was doing something fun. Something to *pass the time*. I hate it when people say *pass the time*, I really do. Time doesn't have to be passed. Time is.

After that they asked her every Sunday, "How are the art classes going?" with a put-on grin and a stupid laugh. Me, I never said much. I knew Gran far too well to piss her off with rubbish chat.

Afterwards, on the way home, Mum and Dad would always nag at me.

"How can you be so rude? You just flop back in your chair. You don't even talk to Gran. She must feel so let down."

Gran feel let down by me? No way! She didn't feel like that! We were a team, Gran and me. We understood each other.

Oh, Mum and Dad were fed up all right. They were really fed up with me. I wasn't clever like my stepsister, Anna. Anna was Mum's daughter from her first marriage. She was five years older than me and she was at Oxford doing Art History and Italian. Yeah, that was great for Anna, but it wasn't for me. Not in a million years.

"She'll end up being a professor," Dad once said, and you could tell how proud he was. Then he looked at me and I knew what he was thinking. My grades were crap. Couldn't he see that I never wanted to be a professor of this or that? I just wanted to get away from school and see the world – go to Australia and America and travel up the Amazon. You don't need crummy certificates on bits of paper and fancy exam grades to do that. Dad had this thing about passing exams. He said I'd get nowhere without good grades. Then the rows started. Mum would nag at me too. In the end, I'd slam the doors to get away from them.

That's when I used to go and see Gran. In those days she had a granny flat in our house. Her flat was warm and untidy and I could just be myself there. Gran never nagged. She was just Gran, sitting by the fire with me and chatting.

"You can be anything you want to be, Chris," she said to me. "Grab the world. It's all out there waiting for you."

That's the sort of talk that filled my head with ideas. Sometimes Gran turned off the light and we'd gaze at the pictures the fire made.

I started seeing the fire-pictures when I was five, when Gran said to me, "Chris, did you know that there's a whole world of stories in a fire?"

“What d’you mean, Gran?”

I remember the way Gran smiled as she poked the fire, making the red coals tumble around in the fireplace.

“Let the flames die back and you’ll see. Fires have hidden stories,” she said. “Now, look and listen.”

And so she told me the stories she could see in the fire until I could see the pictures in those fires too. Fire-pictures that I dreamed about all through my childhood. When I got older the pictures got more exciting. The stories were adventures now.

Then everything began to go wrong.
I knew that Gran was getting old when she started saying weird things. But I didn’t mind her tangled-up memory. In fact, I even tried to help her.

On Thursdays, Gran went out to tea with her friends. When she started to get muddled in the head, I got one of the friends to ring me up so I could help Gran get home. Gran felt ashamed and asked me not to tell Mum and Dad that she got a bit confused about the buses. No way would I tell them!

Later on she just grinned when she saw me coming for her and held onto my arm hard. No big deal. No matter what, she was still my gran.

I knew something was going on when Mum and Dad started whispering. At first, they kept their plans a secret. They'd stop talking when I came into the room. Were they whispering about me? Was I bad? What had I done?

I found out what was going on one Tuesday. I remember it was Tuesday because that was the day I got home late after rugby. I was a fullback – and a bloody good one, too. Mum and Dad were talking in the kitchen. *Now* what had I done? I was sure that they were talking about me. Why else would they stop talking as soon as I came in?

Dad gave a cough. "Chris," he began.

I took a deep breath.

"It's about Gran," he said.

Chapter 2
No Choice

"What?" I let all my muddy gear from rugby practice drop onto the floor. "She's not sick?" I croaked. "She was fine this morning ..."

Mum came over and took my hand. I backed away. Mum wasn't into touching – except when there was heavy stuff to follow.

"She's ... she's not dead, is she?" I whispered. The words choked me. I couldn't bear that. Gran was the only person I trusted. She was my rock.

"No," Dad let out a laugh. "She's not dead at all. It's just ..." he broke off and looked at Mum. He always did that when he couldn't find the right words.

"It's just that her memory has got very bad," put in Mum. "Soon she'll be a danger to herself – wandering off and getting lost in town ..."

"How do you know?" I cut in. I thought I'd kept that secret very well. How did they know I sometimes went to find Gran in town?

"Oh, Chris," Mum went on. "For heaven's sake! Of course we know. It's a small town. People have been telling us about how she forgets where she is sometimes and doesn't know how to get home. Now we have to watch she doesn't go out by herself at night. The time has come when Gran needs full-time care. She needs to go into a Home."

"No!" I cried. "I know what you're saying. But she's only gone out at night twice. And that was because she got day and night mixed up. That's no reason to dump her in a Home. You can't do that. Not to Gran!"

"We've no choice," said Mum softly. "She can't be left alone. I can't be here during the day, neither can your dad ..."

"You're never here, you and Dad," I said. I was angry. What I had said was rude but true. Mum worked long hours for a big legal firm. Dad worked "all the hours God sent" as he said himself, for a big bank. Think posh offices and smart suits, people with all-year suntans and loud, brash voices. Dad's work meant he had to travel abroad a lot. So you can see how both my mum and dad were pretty booked up time-wise.

Which reminds me of the dinner parties. When I was very small, Mum and Dad let me meet their friends. There were pats on the head and cuddles from ladies who smelled of smart perfume. Ugh! But as I got older I was simply sent off to my room. Of course, I always sneaked down to Gran's flat. We used to make toasted cheese sandwiches and eat lots of chocolate.

"Don't you mind?" I asked Gran once.

"Mind what?" she said, licking melted chocolate from round her lips.

"That Mum and Dad don't invite you to those dinners."

Gran laughed so much her false teeth wobbled. "Up there with that lot?" she said in her Irish accent. "I wouldn't fit in at all. Not with all them stuffed shirts and posh frocks."

Both of us knew that Gran wasn't up there with the posh frocks and smart suits because she couldn't talk their talk. She'd left school at 16 and, as she said, she didn't have much to say to people like that.

Chapter 3
Gran Leaves Home

The first time I knew that there was something very wrong with Gran was when we were playing Scrabble.

We had a league going. The first person to win ten games won a pound. We both cheated so nobody ever won the pound.

At first, when her words started to get jumbled up, I thought Gran was into cheating really badly. Not just bad spelling, but rubbish.

She'd get cross and throw up her hands.

"Stupid bloody game."

"Gran!"

Then she'd go quiet and gaze into the fire.

I hoped that when she forgot her words at Scrabble she was just having a bad moment.

After that, the shops in town began to phone and say Gran was wandering about, lost. I had to accept that she'd never be quite the same again.

Of course, it was always me who got the phone calls, because Mum and Dad didn't get home until late. I didn't tell them. They didn't need to know. Not until Gran began to walk out at night.

And now, here were Mum and Dad, talking of putting Gran into a nursing home.

"There's no need," I said, trying to keep my voice steady. "I can look after her. I can, honest. I'll fetch her whenever she wanders off. I always do ..." I broke off.

How stupid could I get! I'd just blown Gran's secret.

Dad shook his head. "It's no good, Chris. She'll be much better off ..."

"She won't! She'll curl up and die. Maybe that's what you want. Maybe you'd like me to curl up and die, too." And I ran to my room. I slammed the door. I punched my pillow.

I felt angry about all sorts of things in my life, not just the problems with Gran.

Mum came up later with some sandwiches. She tried to be kind and talk to me. But I wasn't listening.

In the days before Gran left, I spent every moment I could at home with her.

Once I saw her staring at the fire.

"What are you thinking, Gran?"

Without looking away from the fire, she smiled and said, "Chocolate moon."

"Huh?"

She looked at me and blinked. "Oh, Chris. Just day-dreaming, that's all."

"What's a chocolate moon?"

"Chocolate moon? Did I say that?"

"You did. What is it?"

But Gran just shook her head. "My old memory," she muttered. "It plays tricks."

I didn't ask any further because I could see she was upset.

Dad said that there were times when Gran's mind was normal and she remembered most things. But then, all at once, she'd drift off into a quiet place inside her head.

I wished I could help her hold on to the normal moments, but doing that was like trying to grab a slippery fish. The normal moments just slipped away.

Sometimes Gran even called me Peter, my dad's name. At first I put her right, but that only made her more upset. In the end, I just went along with it.

The day they moved Gran to Saint Mark's Nursing Home, I stayed with my mate, Billy. Billy's mum knew what was going on so she was extra mumsy to me.

"Your gran'll be fine, Chris," she said. "She'll settle down and make new friends."

"I wish she was dead," I snapped back.

Billy's mum looked shocked. What I wanted to say was that if Gran was dead I could mourn for her. I could be sad and remember our special times together. I could say goodbye to her properly.

When I thought of her slipping into a slow death in a strange place, away from home, I felt cold inside.

Chapter 4
Billy Talks Sense

It was Billy who made me snap out of my bad mood.

"Time you got out of it, Chris," he said. "Your gran is old. Shit happens. Life goes on, you know."

"What do you know?" I said angrily. "I hate Sundays. I hate seeing her sitting there ..."

"Yeah, yeah, I know. You told me. You can't talk to her, you feel bad and all that. That's just self-pitying crap, Chris. You're just thinking about how *you* feel. Why don't you get the bus and go by yourself to see her? Cheer up the old dear instead of hanging around like a friggin' zombie."

At first I felt like punching him, but I knew he was right. And that's when I began going to see Gran after school on Wednesdays. We'd sit and chat together in the main lounge of the nursing home. Most times she was OK and we talked just like we used to. Other times she drifted off in her mind to some far-away memory and talked to me about people I didn't know. But I just went along with it and nodded. Except when one time she said Dad's name.

"Poor Peter," she muttered.

"Why 'poor Peter'?" I asked.

Gran blinked and looked at me. "My mind was off wandering again, wasn't it?" I gave a shrug. I didn't know what to say.

"I keep doing that, Chris. I keep slipping away and I can't help it." She curled her fingers into tight, bony fists and shook her head. "It's why they put me here."

"Oh, Gran," I began.

"Shush. It's all right. I know how it is. I'm not stupid. I saw my father go like this, Chris."

She held my hand. "I know what's ahead of me and it scares me. But we must hang on to what we've got. As long as I've got you, my Christ without a T."

"Your what?"

"My helper and saviour," she laughed. "I forgot you're not into religion. Christ helped people and made them feel better. You're the person who helps me and you're Chris – 'Christ without a T'. Anyway, come to my room. I have something for you."

Her room was too neat, but you'd expect that in a nursing home like Saint Mark's. The few bits she'd brought from home looked sad and lost in her new room.

"Here we are," said Gran. She hunted around for something in a chest of drawers. "I want you to have this."

It was her bankcard. Around it was a piece of paper with a number written on it. I backed away.

"I can't take it, Gran. That's your money."

"Take it and shut up," she said firmly and pressed the card into my hand. "I'm going to lose the damn pin number and I don't want anyone else mucking about with my few pounds. They're for you, and I'm giving this to you now while I can see you enjoy it. Not for booze and birds, mind," she added. "Let's just say that from now on you're in charge of my money. If ever I want something special, you'll get it for me, eh?"

I didn't want to but I took the card and tucked it into my pocket. I took the little bit of paper with the pin number on as well.

"You seem to be settling in well, Mum," Dad said to Gran one Sunday. But as he said that, Gran frowned and looked around with fright. It was as if, all at once, she didn't know where she was. Her eyes looked worried and confused. She made me feel scared.

"Can we go now?" she said. "I'll get my coat. Mam is waiting for her tea. Chocolate moon," she muttered. "Chocolate moon." And then she rocked to and fro.

"Dad," I whispered. It was just Dad and me that day. Mum said if all three of us went, it might just confuse Gran.

Dad swallowed hard. "It's all right, Chris," he said. "She'll come back to the present. Just wait a bit."

She did snap back, but we all felt a bit embarrassed and couldn't think of what to say to each other.

"What's a chocolate moon?" I asked Dad in the car on the way home.

"Nothing," he said quickly. "It means nothing."

But I knew by the way he said it that it did mean something to him.

Chapter 5
Chocolate Moon

A few weeks later Gran talked about the chocolate moon again. This time I asked her about it.

"What chocolate moon?" I wanted to know.

She looked at me as if she didn't know who I was.

"It's at home," she said. "My chocolate moon. At home. I want to go there. I have to see my chocolate moon. We'll go now." And she started to get up, out of her chair.

"Gran," I put my hand out to stop her.

She blinked, just like she always did when the normal part of her brain kick-started back into action.

"Talking nonsense, was I, Chris?"

"Yeah," I agreed. "Just a bit."

"Damn it! Will this ever go away?" she cried. She twisted her hands about and looked around in a helpless way. "I can't stand this." Then she saw I was upset. "I'm sorry, Chris. Don't mind me. I'm happy you're here with me."

"No, you're not," I said.

"What?"

"You're not happy at all. When you go back into your head you talk about home and something to do with a chocolate moon."

Gran gave a frown. "Of course I'm happ—"

"No, Gran. That's just an act. Talk to me. Tell me how it is. Tell me now."

She bit her lip, making her false teeth move a bit. "I hate the way I am," she said in a low voice. She seemed to think that if she talked in a whisper she might not slip off into that other world in her head. "And I hate where I'm heading because I know there's no way out. I won't get better. But if I could just see my home one more time ..."

"Of course you can," I cried. "We'll take you home—"

"No, lad," put in Gran. "I mean my real home."

"You mean in Ireland?"

Gran nodded and sighed. "But that's just an old woman's fancy. Now, come on. Let's go and get some tea. They do the best sticky buns here."

I didn't ask her any more about the chocolate moon. One thing at a time.

Chapter 6
Trouble

The big blow-up came after the parent-teacher meeting. I knew I was in trouble when I saw Dad's face.

"You're a disgrace," he said. "A bloody disgrace. You're no good to anyone!"

"Hush, Peter," said Mum. "Let's talk this thing over calmly."

"Calmly?" Dad's voice sounded like thunder. "We've tried all that. We've done the calm talk bit. It looks like it didn't work with Mr Loser here."

"What's your problem?" I said.

I didn't want to listen to him so I turned up the sound on the TV. Stupid move, I know, but it was the only thing I could come up with just then. That made Dad go ballistic. He took the remote from me and threw it across the room. Mum picked it up without any fuss and turned the TV off.

"We'll talk calmly," she said again.

"No, we won't. I can't take any more of this rubbish. Every teacher I spoke to said the same thing – 'Chris could do better'. What sort of nonsense is that? What they mean is that you're a no-good waster."

"Hush, Peter," put in Mum. "That's going a bit far—"

"Far? Far! Not far enough. You're 15, Chris. Isn't it time you thought ahead? Get your act together. In two years' time you'll be trying to get to college ..."

"Oh, here we go again," I groaned. "College and a safe, good job after that. And end up like you, Dad! No time for anything except your cruddy work. Get a life."

"No need to be rude, Chris," said Mum.

"Yes, Mum. There *is* a need to be rude. I've had it up to here with Dad's pushy plans for me. I'm me. I'll decide what I want to be. Please, give me a break."

"Oh, you can have all the breaks you want," snorted Dad. "Why don't you leave right now and sign on with the other losers? And don't think I don't know about you smoking in your room."

"Oh, cut it out, Dad. You're a stuck-up snob. Your head's so far up in the clouds that you've lost touch with reality. But then, maybe you never did catch on to what really matters."

"What do you mean by that?"

"Gran ..."

"Ah, I wondered when that would come out. You blame me for Gran's Alzheimer's, is that it? The fact she's losing her mind?"

Alzheimer's. No-one had ever said the word before. But now that what was wrong with Gran had a name, everything I was feeling started to come out.

"Maybe I do!" I shouted at Dad. "*You* never had time for her, did you? She made you feel embarrassed. Bet you're glad she's safely tucked away now. You couldn't wait, could you? And what about me? I embarrass you too, don't I, Dad? How will you ever tell your golf-club cronies that your son is a drop-out?"

"That's enough, Chris," Mum's voice cut in sharply. "Go to your room and we'll talk when you both calm down. GO NOW!" she shouted as I just stood there, too angry to move.

"I'll go," I muttered. "I've always gone, haven't I? Going to my room has always meant you don't have to talk to me. *You're* the losers."

Dad started to come towards me, but Mum held him back. I didn't hang around. I slammed my door and played loud music. The sort I knew they hated. And that's when I made my plans.

Chapter 7
The Great Idea

Gran was surprised to see me in her room next morning. Surprised and glad. I was glad too, glad to see that she was normal that day.

"Is that your rugby gear?" she asked, pointing to the big sports bag slung over my shoulder.

"No, it isn't, Gran," I said. "I've come to take you away."

"What? You've come to what?"

"Hush. Keep your voice down. I'm taking you to Ireland. I'm taking you home. You said you wanted to see your old home."

"What are you talking about, Chris? Don't talk daft, son."

"I've never been so serious in my life, Gran. I've got some of your money out from the bank. We're going to Ireland."

Her face lit up, just for a moment, and then dulled down again. "Your parents – do they know about this?" she asked. "Are they coming too?"

I shuffled a bit. "It's just you and me, Gran. It's all right. I have it all sorted."

"They don't know then?"

"No. They think I'm going camping with Billy and a few of my mates. See? I've even got my sleeping bag with me."

"That's l... l... begins with l," she said, shaking her head, as she'd been doing lately when the right word couldn't get through.

"Lying? Yeah, just a bit, Gran. Look, we'll be fine. We'll get the train to Fishquard and the afternoon ferry to Ireland. Simple."

"No, Chris. It's a lovely idea, but ..."

"But nothing, Gran. Come on. You've got to do this before ..." I didn't say any more, but Gran understood.

"Before I lose my marbles."

"Whatever," I muttered. "Let's get some of your stuff together. It'll fit in here." I opened the bag. "Don't just sit there looking at me like that. You're wasting time. Where's your sense of adventure, Gran? You were always the one telling me to grab life with both hands. Now we're going to grab a little bit, you and me."

"They'll blame me," she began. "There'll be trouble ..."

"Sod trouble. I'm 15, Gran. I went to France on my own last holidays and I went to see Anna in Italy. I'll look after you. Trust me. You want to see Ireland again – you know you do." I leaned closer to her. "Chocolate moon," I said gently. Her face softened and that far-away look came over her face.

"Chocolate moon," she said softly. Then she blinked alert and gave me a big smile. "Sod it, as you say yourself, Chris. Let's do it."

"Good on you, Gran," I laughed. "We'll have a blast."

We threw some things into the bag and I had her out of the Home before she could change her mind.

"Gran's coming to us for the weekend," I said to the nurse by the main door. "I have a taxi waiting outside."

"Fine, Chris," she said. "Just sign your gran out."

Chapter 8
We Set Sail

"Wales," I said. "We're in Wales now." The train was moving fast through green hills and fields.

Gran looked out the window. "Wales?" she muttered. She didn't seem to know where she might be. But then, she'd been asleep for most of the journey so she was probably a bit muzzy. Please, I begged, please, God, keep her mind working properly.

"Trains," said Gran. "He loved trains."

"Who did?"

She gave me that "hello, stranger" look, as if she didn't know who I was. "Peter. Peter loved trains. We came through Wales then, too."

"When was that?"

She didn't answer my question and went on gazing out the window. "He sat on the table and was so excited. He'd never been on a train before. Poor Peter."

There she was again with the "poor Peter" thing. But I didn't ask why Peter was "poor". I knew by now that too many questions just made her muddled, most of all when she wasn't quite sure where she was. Gran rested her chin on her hand and went on looking out at the houses and little gardens that the train was going past.

"Five," she said, in the end. "He was five. We were going to start a whole new life – away from ... that." She stopped. She looked sad and bitter – in a way I'd never seen before. I didn't like it. But then she smiled to herself and looked at me properly. "I'd really fancy a cup of tea, Chris."

When we reached Fishguard she began to panic. "This is mad," she said as we sat in the big, gloomy waiting area. "I should never have said I'd do this. Your parents—"

"I told you, they think I'm camping. Billy knows. He'll back me up. No turning back now, Gran. Going to see your chocolate moon."

Gran gave a frown and started to fret. "What are you talking about?"

"It's OK," I said gently. "We're doing the right thing. Stop worrying."

It was exciting getting onto the ferry and that made Gran feel better. There weren't many passengers so we could choose where we wanted to sit. We found some seats looking out at the sea. Looking at the waves sent Gran to sleep again. I'd got used to this slipping in and out of dozing – it was part of what was wrong with her. I slipped away to play a few games on the game machines. Bad mistake. When I got back there were some people around Gran, trying to calm her down.

"It's my little boy," she cried, trying to pull away from them. "He's only five. I have to find him."

I pushed through and grabbed her arm. "Excuse me," I said. "She's with me. She'll be fine." They looked at me with surprise. "I'm her grandson and I'm not five," I went on. "She's just got a bit confused. It's OK."

"Well, if you're sure," one of the women said. She wasn't sure what to do for the best so she was glad to hand the old lady over to me.

"Gran, it's me, Chris," I said. I squeezed her hand. Gran looked at me. Her eyes were blank. "Come on, Gran," I snapped. I felt angry with her for all the fuss, but mostly angry with myself because I knew I shouldn't have left her alone. "Get your act together."

She blinked and looked at me. All at once, she saw who I was. "Oh, Chris," she said. "I thought it was me and Peter on this boat, you see. I thought I'd lost him – Peter. We came on the boat together, just him and me."

"Well, you're with me now. Relax."

"Peter was just a little lad," she went on. "He was five when we left home." She looked at me again, her mind clear. "We had to leave."

"Why?"

Gran took a deep breath. "We had to leave because I wasn't married to Peter's dad."

"Wow!" I couldn't believe what Gran had just said. What could I say after that? Something stupid, that's what. "You mean my dad's a bastard?" I said, with a laugh. "Sorry,

Gran," I went on as I saw her face. She looked upset. "I didn't mean ..."

"That's why we've kept it a secret all these years," she said in a soft voice. "People saying stupid things like that. Anyway, you're old enough now to know about it. I can't carry that secret to my grave."

"There are heaps of single mums, Gran." I said. "It's no big deal. Not now."

"It was a big deal back then," muttered Gran. "Most of all in a small, gossipy village. It got too much for me. When my mother died I decided to leave Ireland. I didn't want anybody ever to point a finger at my son and make him feel bad about himself." She looked out at the waves again. "We took the boat to England and I've never been back home. Those waves – it all comes back, Chris. Poor Peter."

Poor Peter – my dad – a bastard. Well, well!

Chapter 9
We Arrive

I sent Billy a text on my mobile to tell him we'd arrived in Ireland. He texted back to say that rain had washed them out of camp and they'd all decided to go home. He added that he'd keep his head down so that my parents wouldn't spot him.

Nice one, Billy. But I knew it was only a matter of time before they'd find out what I'd done. The rest of the gang would be hanging around the shopping centre and Mum would notice them – Friday evening was when she went shopping. Oh, well. I couldn't do anything about it. I had to carry on with my plan now.

"You tired, Gran?" Just my luck if she got ill because she was so tired with all the travelling – from early morning to evening time. I was beginning to think I'd made a big mistake.

"Hm?" Gran kept staring out the window of the bus. "Tired? No, look, it's all so green, just like I remember it."

"You do remember then?"

She turned and looked at me. Her eyes were clear. "Of course I remember. This is my home, isn't it? Those fields haven't changed."

We were just a few miles from Gran's village. She used to tell me about it when I was a kid, so it had been easy to work out how to get there. But now I was beginning to feel worried and with every signpost we passed I felt worse. What if all this ended badly? What if Gran totally lost it when she saw her old place? What if she died of a heart attack?

"Kilross," the bus driver called out as he stopped the bus beside a pub. I made to get up, but Gran put her hand on my arm. What? Had she chickened out?

"Two miles out," she called to the driver.

"Sorry, lady," he called back. "I'm only allowed to stop at proper bus stops. That's the rules."

Gran got in a state. I needed that like I needed a hole in the head.

"She's very old," I said.

The driver gave a shrug. "I don't make the rules," he said. "Sorry."

"Yeah, sure," I muttered.

"It's all right, Chris," said Gran. She got up. "We could do with a bit of a walk after all that sitting."

"Bastard," I said under my breath to the lard-assed driver. But then I thought about how my dad was a bastard in the true sense of the word, and the insult had no meaning any more.

"You sure you can walk two miles?" I asked Gran.

She leaned on my arm and nodded. We walked right the way down the sleepy street. I counted four pubs, a chip shop, a church and a Spar supermarket.

"This shop used to be Murphy's," said Gran, stopping outside the supermarket. "This is where I met your dad's dad."

"Huh?" I waited to see what she would say next.

"Jimmy Murphy. He was the son of the owner. They lived above the shop. He was a skinny young lad with spots on his neck. God, what did I think I was doing? He ran off like a scared rabbit when I told him I was pregnant."

"The creep," I muttered, trying to get my head around what she'd just told me. When you're standing outside the place where your grandad once lived it makes you think hard.

Dad had always told me that his father was a fine fellow who died young. And Gran would never talk about him when I asked. So I had always thought my grandad must have been a handsome, tragic hero who had left them both so heartbroken that they couldn't talk about him. Now I'd found out that he was a skinny, spotty young guy who'd done a runner. I couldn't get my head around it all. It felt like I was looking in on someone else's life.

"His family couldn't take the disgrace," Gran went on. "The shame of him having got a young girl pregnant. His parents sent him off to his uncle in Dublin and I never saw him again. I heard he ended up in America. People said I should've gone too. Been sent off to the nuns to have the baby there and nobody know. Some father, eh, Peter?"

"Chris, Gran. It's Chris."

"I mean Chris," she said. She frowned because she'd forgotten who I was again. "Don't mind me. I get mixed up."

"Listen," I said. "I've got an idea. Why don't I go into that shop and tell them Jimmy Murphy was my grandad and their sad little shop belongs to me. What about it, Gran? Free sausages and beans for the rest of our lives."

That cheered her up. "Do that and I'll slap you around the ears, you cheeky brat," she said with a laugh.

Outside the town a man in a big muddy jeep pulled up beside us.

"Want a lift, folks?"

Boy, were we glad! Gran had been walking more and more slowly. The man pushed a sheepdog into the back of the car and brushed hairs off the front seat.

"Where are you headed?" he asked.

"The Kelly farm," I said, not even sure if Gran was right about it being two miles out of the village. The man turned and looked at me. He was puzzled.

"That place is empty," he said. "Has been for years. Are you sure?"

I looked back quickly at Gran. Her eyes were closed and I knew she was out of it. It was up to me. "Yeah, my gran just wants to have a look. She used to live there years ago."

"Your gran's a Kelly?"

"That's right."

"There's no-one there," he went on. "You'll be wasting your time, lad."

"It's OK. Just drop us off at the gate." Now I was really nervous. What was I doing here in the middle of a strange country, visiting an empty, derelict house with an old lady who thought she was coming back home? And the sun was sinking. I could have kicked myself for not asking about a B&B back at the village. Then, at least, we'd have had somewhere to stay for the night.

Chapter 10
The Old House

The path up to the front door was overgrown with weeds. Gran held my arm tightly as we shuffled through them.

"Home," she said, nodding towards the dark farmhouse ahead. "It always looks so lovely against the sunset."

More like an old dump, I thought. "We'll just have a quick look, Gran," I said. "Then we'll have to get back to the village and find a B&B."

But Gran wasn't listening. Her eyes were focussed on the house.

The downstairs windows were boarded up, but I don't think Gran even noticed that. She had a huge smile and I knew she was in that far-away place inside her head.

I kicked in the front door, scaring a few crows off the roof.

"The hall's a bit of a mess," I said. "Needs a bit of a sweep."

"A bit of a sweep," echoed Gran. She went past me and headed for the stairs.

"Hold on, Gran," I said. "Those stairs could be rotten. Don't ..."

But she was already on her way up. I had no choice but to follow. At least I'd be behind her if she fell.

This was all going so wrong. I hadn't thought the house might be empty and derelict. What had been in my head? Did I think that the house would be owned by some uncles and aunts who'd be happy to see Gran come back? That they'd fuss about and give us hot grub and soft beds? What sort of brain-dead nerd was I?

Gran moved like a zombie along a short corridor upstairs and stopped at a door that was covered with damp stains. She turned round and smiled. But I knew that smile wasn't for me. All of this had sent her back, deeper into the past.

"We're home, Peter," she said. "It's all going to go right for us now, lad."

"Gran! I'm not Peter, I'm Chris." This was going too far and it was my bloody fault. "Get back to the present now, Gran. Please."

No such luck. She went into the room and stopped at the window seat. "Look at that sunset sky," she said.

"Yeah, Gran. It's something else. Now I think we'd better go."

Gran sat on the window seat. The sunset was reflected on her face. She wasn't listening to me. I'd never felt so helpless, or so stupid, in all my life. I sat beside her. I put my hands on her face and turned her face back towards me so she had to look right at me.

"It's me, Gran. It's Chris. Please talk to me."

She blinked. "Of course it's you, Chris. You've brought me home. You're a good lad."

I breathed a sigh of relief. She was normal again. But for how long?

I knew I couldn't shift the old lady. She was here to stay, no matter how I tried to get her to move. I unrolled my sleeping bag and tucked it around her. And I put my baseball cap on her head. She just continued watching the sky turn from pink to deep blue.

"Will you be all right for a few minutes?" I asked.

She didn't answer. Just smiled. I ran down the stairs and found as much old wood as I could – old floorboards, the legs of a rickety table and a few fallen branches from outside.

Gran was still staring out the window when I got back. Not moving.

"Gran!" I shouted.

"What?"

"You ... you OK?"

"Of course, I'm OK. Look," she nodded towards the sky. "It will soon be here."

"What will?"

But Gran was staring at the sky again.

I screwed up the newspaper I'd bought her on the ferry, and built a proper fire in the rusty old fireplace. I thanked my stars I had some matches. I always carry some round in case I get offered a fag. The flames made me feel better and lit up the room as it got darker and darker.

I got Gran away from the window and sat her on my sports bag near to the fire.

"We can still see the sky from here," I said.

"Soon. Here soon," was all she said.

The sandwiches I'd saved from the ferry were a bit soggy, but we ate them anyway. And, though the Mars Bars had melted a bit, they tasted OK and warmed us up.

We sat in silence, except for the crackling of the fire. I didn't say anything to Gran. I knew now I'd lost her to the past and I was too tired to keep trying to pull her mind back to me. After a while, I dozed off.

"There!" Gran's cry jogged me awake.

"What?"

"There, just like always." She was pointing to the window. The sky had got dark, but at the edge of the window a thin thumbnail of light had appeared.

"Remember how we used to sit here, Peter? Remember how it was? You and me at the time we loved the best. Mam in bed and all the nagging shut down for the night. Just you and me. Remember?"

I gulped hard. "Yes."

"No nagging. No pointing fingers. Just you and me waiting. Wait now." Her face was alive. Her eyes glinted in the firelight as she focussed on the window. She watched. I waited. And then there it was – the full moon lighting up the room, casting blue shadows across the bare floorboards.

"Our moon, Peter," she whispered. "Our own chocolate moon."

Chapter 11
Gran's Story

I looked out at the big white ball in the sky. Chocolate? Then I knew what Gran meant. The moon looked just like one of those white chocolate buttons that little kids like. A huge white chocolate button in the sky.

Was this it? Was this why I'd dragged Gran all the way here? Huh, I could have easily bought a bag of the things back home. I groaned and covered my face with my hands. What a waste. And the worst thing was that now that I'd lost Gran to all the thoughts and memories this old dump was bringing back for her.

"All our hopes, Peter," Gran was saying. "All up in that chocolate moon. Remember how we used to sit here and talk about all the things we'd do when we got away? Wishing on our chocolate moon."

She shook her head and gave a sort of a moan. Then she turned and looked at me. And blinked. "Chris?"

"Yeah, it's me, Gran."

"What are we doing here?"

"It's all right, Gran." Whew! Was I glad that she was back – for however short a time! "I brought you home, see?" I went on. "We're looking at the chocolate moon. The one you and Dad – Peter – used to look at."

She frowned and looked out at the moon again. "We did," she said. "That's our magic chocolate moon."

She turned round and looked at me again. She looked upset, as if she was trying to work things out. "But it all went wrong."

"What?"

She faced the moon again. "Going away with you to England was the happiest time of my life. I swore that you could have anything you wanted – and be anything you wanted to be."

OK, so I was Peter again. I was getting used to the way Gran was by now. It was all part of her Alzheimer's – the way her mind went to and fro between the past and present. I knew about Alzheimer's because I'd looked it up on the net.

I waited for her to go on talking.

"Work," she said. "I worked all the hours God sent" (where had I heard that before!) "to have the very best for you. Waitress by day and office cleaner in the evening. Collect you from the childminder and be too tired to play with you.

"I thought ..." She broke off and began to sway to and fro. "I thought if I got you through school and into college that would be the best thing a mother could do."

She stopped and watched the flames for a moment.

"But it wasn't, was it, Peter? The only good times we had together were when we were sitting here, wishing on our chocolate moon. The rest was just ... just empty.

"I spent too much time making money to give you a real chance in life, and we missed out on our time together. Time is the most important thing."

She began to sway to and fro again, muttering, "Too late, too bloody late."

When my friends said stuff like that I thought it was just slushy crap. But this time it was my own gran talking and what she said made sense.

I tried to imagine Dad when he was a kid, wishing on a white chocolate moon with his mum. And I began to see why he was so pushy for me. Dad had been pushed up and away by his mum. And his mum then gave *me* all her love because she'd screwed up on her own son.

Now Dad was doing to me what she'd done to him. He didn't know any better.

"Jeez, Gran," I muttered.

She had fallen asleep after all that talking. The last of the moon slipped behind a cloud. The firelight sent flickering shadows around the bare room. I couldn't see any pictures in that fire to cheer me up.

I dug around in my coat pocket and fished out my mobile. I wanted to talk to my dad. I needed to.

"Dad?" I said. The line was awful. "Dad, I'm with Gran in her old home. We're all right. Don't worry." The line crackled. I didn't even know if he'd heard me.

Chapter 12
Dad

I was worn out from trying to keep the fire going. Gran was fast asleep. I got her properly into the sleeping bag and put the bag of clothes under her head like a pillow. The moon had vanished long ago, and the lonely sounds of night animals were giving me the creeps. Give me the noise of city life – the whole country-life thing does my head in.

"This was a mad idea, Gran," I whispered. "All I've done is push you right into that cruddy Alzheimer's. My own stupid fault."

Each time my eyelids got heavy, I pulled myself awake. If I didn't keep that fire going all night long, we'd freeze. I'd heard about old people dying from the cold. Trying to keep Gran alive and warm was making me panic.

Sleep was just about to win its battle when I saw lights flash across the room. All at once I was awake. *Please let that flash not be real!* But then I heard soft voices below and the shuffle of footsteps. My heart beat madly. I grabbed a bit of wood and stood beside Gran. She was still fast asleep.

The footsteps were coming up the stairs now. Junkies, I thought. The footsteps must belong to junkies. Out to shoot up their fixes in a derelict house. How many people were there? They wouldn't want to find Gran and me here. I held on to the bit of wood tightly. The door opened and a flashlight dazzled me.

"Come one step closer and I'll smash your heads in," I said in a low voice.

"Put that stick away, lad," said the voice behind the torch. "It's the police."

I didn't know what to do. "We're not doing any harm," I shouted. "We ... this is my granny's old home ..."

"We know. Now put down that stick and relax."

"You know?"

"Your father rang us up. He was worried."

Dad! My own father had shopped me to the cops.

"I only took her to see her old house," I said. "There was no harm ..."

"Wake up your granny, lad. We're taking you away from here."

"Where?" I asked. "Look, there's no need to put us in the nick. This is Gran's old home.

We're not doing any harm. Told you that, didn't I?"

The other policeman gave a laugh.

"The nick is it? Do you think we're putting you away for the night? No, kid. We've found somewhere for you to stay – in a B&B. Your father asked us to do that. Now wake the lady up. She'd be scared if one of us tried to."

Gran was very upset when I woke her. She didn't know where she was, and she was cold. I tried to calm her down, but it was all too much. Being woken up, seeing the torches and the two hefty policemen sent her into a panic. It took both of them to calm her down and half carry her to the car.

The woman at the B&B fussed about us – well, she fussed about Gran, giving her tea and toast. She didn't seem to like me at all. She knew what I'd done. I felt a right twit.

"Your dad's getting a plane from England as soon as he can," one of the policemen said. "He'll be here to take you home tomorrow. Don't worry," he said with a grin when he saw my tense face, "I expect he'll give you an earful, but the main thing he wanted to know was if you were all right."

Yeah, right. So that was why he'd got the police onto me.

"We were OK," I muttered. "We were fine." But even while I was saying it I knew that I was talking rubbish. If I'd been younger I'd have started blubbering by now.

"Get some sleep," said the second policeman. "It will all seem better tomorrow."

Of course I didn't sleep. I tossed about all night as I thought about Dad coming and what he'd say. There was just too much in my head for me to relax. Much later a knock on the door woke me up. Dad? I wanted to lie down and die. But it was Mrs Brown, the owner of the B&B.

"Your granny's asking for you," she said. "She's a bit confused, I think."

Well, that got me moving. Gran was sitting on the side of her bed, trying to put her shoes on. "Ah, Chris," she said. Her face lit up. She knew me. That was a relief.

We spent the day walking round the village. Gran remembered some places and had totally forgotten others. Sometimes she knew who I was, sometimes she didn't. But all in all she seemed to be having a good time. Mrs Brown fussed again and made us another big meal. But I could only pick at it.

It was late evening when Dad arrived in a hired car. Mrs Brown showed him into her sitting room. Dad and I looked at each other slowly. He went right over to Gran. He didn't say anything, just held her very close.

“Peter,” said Gran, over and over. “Peter.”

I felt left out. In fact I was jealous of the way she clung to Dad, not wanting to let go.

“Mum, I’ve come to take you home – take you back,” he added quickly. After all she was “home”. “I have flights booked for tonight.”

He still didn’t speak to me. Saving it all for a proper shoot-out, no doubt.

Gran looked up at him. “We came on the boat, Peter,” she said, as Dad helped her into the back of the car. “You remember the boat? You were such a little lad.”

Dad nodded. “I remember.”

“Such a wild little lad.”

We drove through Kilross. Gran was lost in her thoughts – wherever they were. I wished Dad would say something, yell at me, anything. The air was tense. No-one said a word. Gran sat on her own in the back and I sat next to Dad in the front.

As we left the village and drove into the open countryside, the full moon loomed in front of us.

"Our chocolate moon," said Gran softly from the back seat. "See, Peter?"

"We have a chocolate moon in England too, Mum," said Dad. But as he spoke, he looked over at me.

"That's right, Gran," I said and I turned round to see her. But her eyes were closed. I wished they weren't. I needed her to talk. Dad and me, we were both so tense. When would Dad get round to shouting at me?

He did say something after a while. "Fish and chips for three, Chris?"

"Yeah, Dad, that would be good."

I knew then that Dad and me had got a bit closer to each other. There was a pinch of hope that he might not be too angry. That he'd turn into an OK bloke.

"Gran will be OK, won't she?" I asked.

Dad didn't say anything at first. After all, he'd just had to go back to where he'd lived when he was little and remember a whole lot of stuff from when he was a child – good and bad. "She'll still see her white chocolate moon through her new window," he said softly at last.

"Maybe it doesn't matter where Gran is, Dad," I said. "All that dreamy stuff and living in the past, that's her real world now, huh?"

He nodded. "Yes, but we can still be part of it," he said.

Maybe it was that moon, or maybe it was just me, but it felt like a fog was lifting from my head. Life hadn't stopped, it was just going another way. We'd be OK.

"Quick, Dad, get ready to stop," I said. "Chip shop ahead."

Barrington Stoke would like to thank all its readers for commenting on the manuscript before publication and in particular:

Gemma Bain
Louise Barrett
Liz Bridge
Gillian Cunningham
Georgina Harrold
Patricia Hek
Greg Johnston
Shannon Kennedy
Gary Mitchell
Gemma Pryce
Emma Roberts
Michael Saxby
David Scaife
Jenny Stewart
Peter Turner
Corinne Walker
Jill Wharrier
Oliver Wilcox

Become a Consultant!

Would you like to give us feedback on our titles before they are published? Contact us at the address below – we'd love to hear from you!

Barrington Stoke, Sandeman House, Trunk's Close,
55 High Street, Edinburgh EH1 1SR
Tel: 0131 557 2020 Fax: 0131 557 6060
Email: info@barringtonstoke.co.uk
Website: www.barringtonstoke.co.uk

If you loved this book, why don't you read ...

Second Chance

by Alison Prince

ISBN 1-842991-94-9

Ross's noisy family has been thrown out again. This time there's nowhere to go – except the old café on the beach. But odd things have happened there. Who is the boy watching Ross? Watching, and waiting?

If you loved this book why don't you read ...

Walking with Rainbows

by Isla Dewar

ISBN 1-842991-30-2

When Briggsy turns up at Minnie's school on that first Monday in April, Minnie knows he's not like the other boys. Briggsy's family travels with the fairground and he has never stayed in one place for very long. He may have missed out on school but he has learnt what life's all about. He shares his passions with Minnie, and she knows that time spent with Briggsy is going to change her life for ever.